THAUMATURGY ROSEWOOD

NAISHA SAHNI

For the friendship that blooms like roses and shines like magic. <3

Contents

Foreword

When I first sat down to write, I had no idea how much this story would shape me. What started as a simple idea- 3 friends, magic, and an ancient villain- quickly became the world I didn't want to leave.

Stories have always been a part of my life, whether through books, films, or the imagination that fuels daydreams. Writing this book was a leap of faith, one filled with late nights, moments of doubt, and bursts of excitement when everything finally clicked.

My hope is that as you turn the pages, you feel the same sense of wonder that I felt while creating this world. Whether you're here for the adventure, the magic, or the friendships, I welcome you to this journey.

Thank you for being part of it.
- Naisha Sahni

Preface

Writing THAUMATURGY ROSEWOOD, has been an unforgettable journey—one filled with challenges, excitement, and the thrill of crafting a world beyond reality.

The idea first sparked from a simple thought: What if magic had been lost, waiting to be rediscovered? From that question, the characters took shape, the conflicts deepened, and the adventure unfolded. Along the way, I learned that stories have a life of their own, growing in ways I never expected.

This book is for those who believe in the power of imagination. Whether you're here for the mystery, the friendships, or the magic, I hope you find something within these pages that stays with you.

Thank you for embarking on this journey with me.

- Naisha Sahni

Acknowledgements

To my family, thank you for always cheering me on. To my friends, for listening to endless book updates and pretending to be interested—your patience is unmatched. To my beta readers, who made sure I didn't completely lose my mind.

To the authors who came before me, whose stories inspired my own, and to the readers who give books their magic—this one is for you.

And, of course, a special thanks to coffee. I couldn't have done it without you.

PROLOGUE

The bracelet had been hidden for centuries, locked away beneath stone and spell, waiting. Forgotten by time, it carried the remnants of an old curse—the kind that refused to fade.

When the three girls stumbled upon it, they had no idea what they had awakened. The air shimmered, ancient whispers curling in the shadows. Somewhere, deep within the unseen folds of history, magic stirred.

And far beyond their reach, something else awoke. A force long buried, waiting to return.

PLAYLIST

1. *Runaway - Aurora*

2. *Ilahi- Arijit Singh*

3. *Control - Halsey*

4. *Warriors - Imagine dragons*

5. *The Nights - Avicii*

6. *O mahi - Arijit Singh*

7. *Believer - Imagine dragons*

8. *Aayat - Arijit Singh*

THAUMATURGY ROSEWOOD

MANYA, VANSHIKA & NAINA

*Once upon a time in the heart of India, where ancient myths whispered through **bustling** streets and the scent of monsoon rain carried the echoes of forgotten legends, lived a fearless teen named Manya. By her side were Vanshika and Naina, more than best friends, they were sisters in spirit, bound by an unbreakable bond stronger than time itself.*

*Together, they **thrived** on adventure, solving mysteries that others overlooked, turning ordinary moments into thrilling quests. But what started as harmless games soon **spiraled** into something far greater, something beyond their wildest dreams.*

*For fate had **woven** them into a story much older than they could imagine, a tale buried deep within the lost history of Thaumaturgy Rosewood; a place where magic slept, waiting to be awakened. And these three friends were about to **stumble** upon secrets that would change their lives forever..........................*

I
The Mysterious Portal

Summer vacation had officially begun, and the air **buzzed** with excitement. The streets were alive with the scent of roasting corn, the calls of street vendors, and the chatter of children freed from school routines. Naina, Vanshika, and Manya sat **sprawled** across the rooftop of Manya's house, planning their first big party of the season.

"We need decorations, snacks, and definitely a playlist," Naina said, scribbling ideas into her notebook.

Manya leaned back on her elbows, "First, we need something cool, something that makes this party unforgettable."

Naina's eyes sparkled with mischief. "Let's visit Yashvi's antique store. She always has something unique."

Yashvi's shop was unlike any other. Tucked between an old bookstore and a spice shop, the place smelled of ancient wood and secrets. Shelves were stacked with mysterious objects. Things that **hummed** with history, things that whispered forgotten stories.

And only three people in the world knew Yashvi's truth: she wasn't just a collector; she was a **sorceress.**

As they stepped inside, Yashvi greeted them with a **knowing smile.** "Looking for something special? Just yesterday, I received an entire truckload of new treasures; each piece **brimming** with untold stories. Who knows what mysteries lie within?" Vanshika and Manya exchanged excited glances, "We'd love to see the them..."

"Come on then, follow me," Yashvi replied with a knowing smile, leading them down a narrow hallway.

The storage room was like stepping into another era a world of forgotten treasures and mysteries waiting to be uncovered. The dim lighting cast soft shadows over shelves lined with ancient jewellery, mystical orbs, centuries-old books, towering chandeliers, and even an **eerie glass case** holding what looked suspiciously like a preserved mummy. The air smelled of aged **parchment** and incense, thick with history.

As the girls wandered, Manya's **gaze** landed on a delicate bracelet, a gleaming piece with an intricate design, holding what seemed like a **fragment** of something larger. A strange pull made her fingers trace its surface, and just as she turned it over, she spotted two more; each with a similar, incomplete shape.

Something about it felt... important. "These are perfect," she murmured, picking up all three. A wide grin spread across her face as she turned to her friends. "I'm getting these for us." After that Naina & Manya went to their homes to inform their parents about the night stay at Vanshika's house.

Later that evening, the three gathered at Vanshika's house for a long-awaited sleepover. Laughter filled the air as they danced to their favourite songs, watched movies with bowls of popcorn scattered around, and sang at the top of their lungs. As the night deepened and conversations **drifted** toward dreams and adventures, Manya pulled out the three bracelets.

"I got these for us," she said, handing one to each of her best friends.

Vanshika admired the delicate design, her fingers tracing the **intricate** patterns. "This is absolutely gorgeous, Manya. Thank you!"

"I'm in love with it!" Naina grinned, fastening the bracelet onto her wrist. "But wait; can you both hand me yours for a minute?"

Curious, Vanshika and Manya passed their bracelets to her. Naina carefully **aligned** the three pieces, clicking them together to form a perfect heart.

The second they connected; the **air thickened** with energy. A **radiant** sphere emerged between them, its glow pulsing like a heartbeat. Inside, streams of electricity intertwined with flickers of shimmering magic, **swirling** in **hypnotic** patterns. The light grew brighter, until suddenly, the space beside their bed **warped**.

A portal, **rippling** like liquid gold, materialized in the room. Its edges shimmered, revealing glimpses of something beyond, a world unknown, waiting.

"Uh... did I just do that?" Naina whispered, eyes wide with disbelief.

And then, she appeared...

II

An Unknown Guest

From within the portal, a figure emerged, a girl, seemingly in her late 20s. Her dark curls bounced as she stumbled forward, catching herself just in time before she could fall to the floor. She looked both excited and **astonished**, her eyes **darting** around the unfamiliar surroundings.

"I'm here," the girl whispered to herself, voice trembling with emotion. Then, realizing she wasn't alone, she quickly straightened up and **brushed off** the faint glow of magic that still **lingered** on her clothes.

Naina stepped forward cautiously. "Nice to meet you?" she said **hesitantly**, unsure how else to greet someone who had literally fallen from another dimension.

The girl's lips trembled, and, to everyone's shock, tears **welled up** in her large, expressive eyes. "How do I express my gratitude toward you guys?" she sobbed, her voice raw and overflowing with relief. "I was cursed... trapped for so long... I was stuck in the heart of your bracelet."

All three girls exchanged **bewildered** glances, their eyes falling **instinctively** on the bracelet that lay on the table, its **gemstone** flickering faintly.

"You what?" Manya asked, leaning in with intense curiosity. "You were inside the bracelet?"

Mini nodded, sniffing and wiping her tears away. "Yes... my name is Mini, and I lived in a place called *Thaumaturgy Rosewood*."

The name sent **shivers** down Manya's spine. It sounded ancient, mysterious, magical. "Thaumaturgy Rosewood?" she echoed. "That sounds straight out of a fantasy novel. What kind of place is that?"

Mini took a deep breath, her expression **darkening** as she tried to gather herself. "It's a **realm** where magic flows through every leaf, every stone, every heartbeat. But it is also a place of danger. I was betrayed... **accused**... cursed."

Manya's eyes gleamed. "Oo, it's so interesting! I think this bracelet ended up in the right hands. Now, please share the whole story with us!"

Vanshika, ever the practical one, looked around at her friends. "Guys, this sleepover is getting way more interesting than I expected. But before we start unravelling this magic mystery... Mini, would you like to eat something? I bet you must be starving!"

Mini hesitated, as if unsure whether food was something she still needed after her time trapped in the bracelet. But the scent of warm pizza on the table made her stomach **growl**, and she let out a small laugh. "That... would actually be amazing."

With that, the girls eagerly sat together, plates full, ready to dive into a story unlike any they had ever heard before.

Mini: The Story Begins...

In the heart of an enchanted land, hidden beyond **mortal** eyes, lay a kingdom known as Thaumaturgy Rosewood. It was a place where magic was woven into the very fabric of existence, where the rivers sang, the trees whispered ancient spells, and the air itself shimmered with mystical energy.

I lived there with my sister, Yashvi, in a family destined for greatness. We were the *Guardians of Rosewood*, protectors of all magic, **sworn** to ensure that its power was never misused or **tainted** by greed. Our days were filled with adventure, discovery, and the joy of **wielding** magic that pulsed through our veins.

But happiness is a fragile thing.

One day, the darkest force in history set his gaze upon our kingdom—the ruthless and powerful Sorcerer, Veyron. He was feared across galaxies, known for his **insatiable** thirst for domination. And now, he desired the most precious jewel of Thaumaturgy Rosewood, our princess, *Mohini.*

Veyron did not seek love, nor companionship. His proposal was **laced** with **menace,** for he knew that if he claimed Princess Mohini as his bride, he would gain absolute control over the magic of our realm. With her at his side, he could rule entire galaxies.

One fateful afternoon, his Messenger arrived in the grand halls of the palace, his voice echoing like the toll of a death bell.

"The Princess of Thaumaturgy Rosewood, Lady Mohini, is hereby informed that the greatest of the great, the formidable Sorcerer, Veyron, is in love with her and wishes to take her as his bride. Princess, you have but two choices:- accept his proposal willingly, or **defy** *him, in which case he will annex your power, your magic, and your kingdom. If you* **resist,** *he will imprison you, leaving your land and people at his mercy."*

A suffocating silence hung in the air. The weight of the **ultimatum** was unbearable.

Princess Mohini rose from her throne, her eyes burning with defiance. *"I will never bow to a tyrant. I reject this proposal. If Veyron believes we will surrender without a fight, then he knows nothing of Thaumaturgy Rosewood. We do not* **yield.** *We do not fear. If war is what he seeks, war is what he shall receive."*

The declaration of war thundered across the land.

Darkness came swiftly. Veyron unleashed his army. Legions of cursed beings, shadows that moved like ghosts, creatures **forged** from nightmares. Magic clashed against magic. Fire **raged,** storms roared, and the once-peaceful kingdom drowned in chaos.

My family fought valiantly, but one by one, they fell. My sister *Yashvi* vanished, lost in the **mayhem.** I was the last one standing, fighting until my very last breath.

Veyron, his eyes brimming with greed, was willing to go to any extent to annex the magic of Thaumaturgy Rosewood, His insatiable hunger for power made him ruthless, unstoppable. I fought fiercely, channelling every **ounce** of magic within me, pushing my limits as my energy flickered like a dying flame.

The battle raged on, my strength waning with each strike. But just when it seemed hopeless, they arrived; _the Ancient Protectors_.

Warriors of wisdom, their presence radiating an unshakable aura. They were unlike anyone I had ever seen, twice my age, yet wielding magic with an intensity I could barely **comprehend**. Their mere arrival made the battlefield tremble, as if the very ground recognized their power.

Without hesitation, they **confronted** Veyron, their combined forces weaving spells older than time itself. A surge of light enveloped him; an incantation whispered in voices that resonated through the very fabric of existence. He screamed, his monstrous form twisting and **contorting** under their command, until within moments; he was sealed away, trapped in a prison of magic so ancient that only they knew its location.

I barely had time to process it. The Ancient Protectors had won—they had done what I could never have done alone. But before I could even utter a word, they simply vanished.

Gone. As if they had never existed.

For a **fleeting** moment, I believed the war was finally over. We had won.

And then, everything shattered.

From the shadows, _Demetria_, Veyron's most trusted soldier, stepped forward. I had underestimated her. With a single, **precise** strike, she cursed me, her spell **unravelling** everything I had left.

Pain, unlike anything I had known, surged through me. My vision blurred, my body weakened. I could no longer fight back. The battlefield faded, my screams swallowed by the cruel spell that bound me.

Then darkness.

Silence.

And when I woke, I was no longer in Thaumaturgy Rosewood.

I was here; trapped inside the heart of your bracelet. Waiting. Hoping.

Until now.

Naina: OMG! I seriously cannot believe it. This is incredible! But—your sister? Yashvi?! Do you have any pictures of her?

Mini: I do have one. (She reaches into her satchel and pulls out an old, slightly worn photograph. As she holds it up, the dim light in the room catches its edges, revealing a faint shimmer—a trace of magic still lingering in its fibres.)

Naina: (Gasping, eyes widening in shock.) Guys... you won't believe this. Look.

(She passes the picture to Manya and Vanshika, who lean in eagerly. The moment their eyes land on the image, their jaws drop.)

Manya/Vanshika: Oh. My. God!

Manya: (**Heart racing**, voice trembling slightly.) I think... I think we know exactly who she is.

Mini: (**Snapping** her head up, her hands shaking slightly as she **clutches** the bracelet.) You do?! How? Where is she?!

III

The Sisters' Reunion

The **dawn** had barely broken when the girls tiptoed through the quiet corridors of their home, their hearts pounding with excitement and nervous energy. Mini, now free from the **confines** of the cursed bracelet, followed closely behind, her steps light but hesitant. This would be the first time she was going to meet her sister after years of separation, and she wasn't entirely sure how Yashvi would react.

As they approached Antique Shop, the air buzzed with magic. Yashvi sat on an aged wooden chair, absorbed in a newspaper where the images moved—people waving, laughing, and sometimes even stepping out of their frames before returning to their printed positions. The girls gasped at the **surreal** sight.

Naina stepped forward, her voice warm. "Hello, Yashvi. How are you today?"

Yashvi glanced up, **startled** by their sudden arrival. She folded her newspaper, setting it aside with curiosity. "I'm well, but what are you all doing here this early?" she asked, eyebrows raising slightly.

Manya, brimming with excitement, nudged Vanshika. "Well, every time we visit, you have surprises and gifts for us. Today, we have one for you."

Yashvi's curiosity deepened. "Really?! What is it?"

Vanshika took a deep breath before calling, "Come in, Mini into an eerie silence as Mini stepped inside. The moment Yashvi's eyes landed on her long-lost sister, she froze, disbelief **etched** across her face. Her lips parted, yet no words escaped them. Tears welled in her eyes as she stood rooted to the spot, struggling to process the miracle before her.

"Hello there, sis," Mini whispered, voice **tinged** with emotion. "Long time, I suppose."

Yashvi gasped, then, unable to contain herself, rushed forward and embraced Mini with overwhelming affection. "I thought you had died in that war! I ran away, trying to build a new life here. But how—how are you alive? And how do you know these girls?"

Manya, still **elated** from the revelation, beamed. "We freed her from the bracelet we bought from you yesterday!"

Yashvi stepped back, her fingers trembling as she held Mini's shoulders. "But... how is that possible? How were you stuck in that bracelet?"

Mini exhaled slowly. "I was cursed by Dementria, trapped in that piece of jewellery for years. But these wonderful girls freed me. Their friendship was pure, their hearts kind, and that broke the spell."

Yashvi wiped her tears and turned toward the girls, admiration filling her gaze. "I don't know how to thank you. You have returned to me the most precious gem of my life."

Manya waved a hand **dismissively**, smiling. "Oh, no need for that! That's what friends are for!"

The shop filled with joyous chatter as they embraced the moment. Mini stayed by Yashvi's side, assisting her with the mystical artifacts around the shop, reconnecting with her past and relishing the newfound freedom. But unknown to them, their act of kindness had consequences far beyond their understanding.

As Mini's curse had broken, so had the **shackles** of many others, one of whom was The Veyron, an ancient being who had now risen from the depths of darkness.

-----*The Morning of Magic*-----

The next day, the girls arrived **promptly** at The Antique Store, the excitement from the previous day still fresh in their hearts. Vanshika pushed open the wooden door, sending a soft **chime** through the store.

"Good morning, everyone!" she called cheerfully.

Mini, who had been arranging spell books on a shelf, turned with a bright smile. "Good morning! You girls arrived at just the right moment. You know when I was in the bracelet, trapped the _Will of Damico_ appeared and it stated that whoever would free me from the bracelet would be the next ones to be the protectors. Since you freed me from the bracelet's curse, it's my duty to teach you magic.

The words hung in the air like a spell, vibrating with the weight of promise.

"But mini what is the Will of Damico?" Naina asked curiously.

"The Will of Damico is said to be the letter of superior. It only appears when it has to give the most important message. No one knows where it comes from or where it vanishes. It is considered the purest form and sacred in Thaumaturgy Rosewood."

"So, are we ready to learn some magic?" Mini said winking.

Manya clasped her hands together, excitement radiating from her face. "I would love to learn magic!"

Vanshika nodded enthusiastically. "Me too!"

Mini chuckled, pleased by their eagerness. "Then let's begin.

But first! an important lesson: magic is not just about casting spells or waving wands. It comes from within, from our deepest intentions. The truest magic is woven with kindness, courage, and wisdom."

Yashvi, standing near a counter filled with enchanted **trinkets**, smirked. "I suppose I'll be seeing some fiery disasters when you girls try your first spell!"

The girls laughed, but Mini continued with a serious expression. "There is much to learn, and not all magic is light and simple. With spells come responsibilities, and with power, danger. There are forces in this world that seek chaos, lurking in the shadows. We must prepare ourselves."

Manya tilted her head. "Wait are you saying something evil might be out there?"

Mini nodded solemnly. "Yes. When my curse broke, I felt the tremors of magic elsewhere. Something ancient and dark has awakened. We may not know what it is yet, but we must be ready when it finds us."

A hush fell over the room as realization dawned upon them. Their adventure had just begun, but they weren't simply learning magic for fun—they were about to step into the unknown, into a world where myths were real, and legends breathed.

The girls exchanged glances, their nervousness replaced with determination.

Vanshika took a deep breath, then grinned. "Well, if danger is coming, then we better make sure we're strong enough to face it! Let's get started, Mini. Teach us everything you know!"

Mini smiled, her heart swelling with pride. This was more than friendship. It was fate.

"First you will be needing your wands".

IV
Girls and Magic

A **swirl** of golden light **erupted** as a magical portal opened before the girls. Their excitement was **palpable** as they stepped through, entering *THE BOLLIWANDERS*, the most prestigious wand shop in the magical **realm.** The scent of ancient wood and enchanted dust filled the air, and shelves lined with mystical wands stretched far beyond what the eye could see.

Behind the counter stood *Mr. Sunny*, the seasoned wand-maker, **meticulously** examining a rare piece of enchanted wood. As his eyes lifted, they met Mini's, and time seemed to **halt** for a brief moment.

"Mini!" Sunny gasped, eyes widening in shock and joy. "After all these years! how are you here?!"

Mini grinned playfully, stepping forward. "Hello, old friend. How have you been?"

Sunny shook his head in disbelief before breaking into a hearty smile. "Better now! It's been far too long. I suppose these remarkable young ladies helped you escape from that cursed bracelet?"

Mini nodded. "Indeed, they did. And now, I need your help. Just as you gifted me a wand—" she paused, a mischievous **glint** in her eyes, "—about 120 years ago. I need you to provide them with their own wands."

Sunny nearly dropped the piece of wood he was holding. "You're 120 years old?!" Vanshika exclaimed, her eyes wide with astonishment.

Mini winked. "Age is but a number, my dear. We are given anti-aging potion to keep us fit and we continue to protect the realm. Now, Sunny, let's begin."

Sunny chuckled, composing himself. He turned to Vanshika first. "Step forward, young one. Let me see what wand calls to you."

Vanshika took a nervous step toward the counter, her hands clasped tightly together. Sunny studied her carefully, his old, wise eyes reading beyond her features—he saw her courage, her resilience, her fiery determination.

He reached under the counter and pulled out an **ornate** box. The moment he lifted the lid, a deep red light shimmered within.

"*Here, 9.5 inches, *Pegasus heartstring core*, crystal red in color—*the wand of the Mist*. A perfect match for someone like you. Now, try a spell. Flying objects respond well to this wand. Say: Leviosa Ascendio."

Vanshika swallowed nervously before lifting her wand and taking a deep breath. "Leviosa Ascendio!"

A book from the nearest shelf trembled before gracefully lifting into the air. It hovered for a few moments before slowly descending back onto the wooden surface.

She gasped. "This is amazing!"

Sunny smiled. "You have a natural touch. Now, Naina, step forward."

Naina approached with steady steps, her heart pounding in her chest. Sunny observed her closely before nodding in approval.

"Passionate, kind-hearted, innovative... impressive. Your wand must be equally special." He pulled out another elegant box, opening it with reverence. Inside, a soft glow of crystal shimmered.

"Here, 10 inches, *unicorn heartstring core*, crystal yellow in colour. This wand, *the Belle*, is **attuned** to you."

Naina accepted the wand carefully, feeling its warmth seep into her fingertips.

Before Sunny could even call upon Manya, she sprang forward with impatience. "Now my turn, please! I can't wait any longer!"

Sunny chuckled. "Very well, let's see…" He narrowed his eyes, analysing her essence. "Self-assured, extroverted, adaptable… Ah! I know exactly what you need."

This time, he reached for a larger box, lifting its lid to reveal an exquisite, shimmering blue wand.

"12.5 inches, *aqua drop core*, crystal blue in colour—I present you *the Aqua*."

Manya took the wand eagerly, turning it in her hands with fascination. "Beautiful!"

Mini smiled warmly. "These wands are perfect, Sunny. Thank you. Girls, now that you have your wands, it's time to train in magic and protection. We have much to prepare for."

Vanshika **beamed**. "These wands are incredible!"

Manya grinned. "Absolutely! Let's get started."

The girls stood at the threshold of a new destiny, their fingers curling around their newly gifted wands, tingling with possibility. The air shimmered with enchantment, and before them stood Mini, the wise and **enigmatic** mentor of the Magical Court.

Her presence was a gift of guidance, her eyes brimming with ancient knowledge and quiet amusement at the nervous excitement crackling in her students.

Their journey began with the first lesson—a whisper of incantations and flicks of the wrist that could bend the elements to their will. Mini taught them not just the technical mastery of spells, but the profound understanding of magic itself. Magic, she told them, was more than power; it was responsibility, intention, and balance. It required wisdom beyond mere skill.

Each girl had her own unique strengths.

Vanshika, fiery and determined, wielded magic with the precision of a warrior. Her defensive spells were impeccable, creating barriers that no darkness could penetrate.

Manya, gentle and **intuitive**, specialized in healing magic, her energy suffused with warmth that could mend wounds both physical and emotional.

Naina, the strategist, saw magic as a puzzle—her keen mind crafted illusions and protective enchantments with dazzling complexity. Together, they formed a team unlike any the Magical Court had seen before.

Challenges arose swiftly. Dark forces that threatened the kingdom whispered from the shadows. The girls encountered rogue magic—spells gone **awry**, ancient curses left unchecked, and creatures lurking in the depths of forbidden woods.

Each battle tested their courage, forcing them to rely not just on their own abilities, but on each other. Their trust in one another deepened, the bonds of friendship woven tightly through trial and triumph.

But as their powers grew, so did their doubts. Could they wield such immense magic without losing themselves? Mini guided them through these moments of uncertainty, reminding them that true protectors were not those who never feared, but those who faced fear head-on, undeterred.

Their final test came with the threat of an approaching storm—one unlike any they had seen before. It was an **omen** of chaos, a force that sought to unravel the magic of the court itself. It called upon everything they had learned: their spells, their strategy, and their unwavering unity.

As they stood together, wands raised, hearts steady, they knew the truth—magic was not just about fighting battles. It was about preserving hope.

They wielded their power not for destruction, but for the light it could bring. They had transformed, not just as magicians, but as guardians of all that was good and just. Their journey was only beginning, but they stepped forward into it with certainty.

For they were ready. They were the PROTECTORS of magical court.

Now came the harsh part for they had to leave their homes and go with mini to Thaumaturgy Rosewood until they feel that everything is perfect.

Mini had to erase Naina, Manya and Vanshika's parents' memory.

Their heart broke but they promised themselves to come back as soon as possible. Mini put a protection spell on their parents so no evil could harm them.

V
Protectors of the Magical Court

The two years flew by in a **whirlwind** of magic, challenges, and intense learning. The girls mastered spells, honed their abilities, and grew into formidable witches, prepared to protect the realm.

Today was a **momentous** occasion—it was the day they would be officially registered in the Magical world as protectors.

They stood in Mini's enchanted home, the excitement in the air nearly tangible. "One hour left until we teleport to the ceremony!" Vanshika declared, checking the magical clock floating nearby.

Suddenly, a shimmer of dark energy flickered across the room. The girls turned in confusion as an ancient-looking diary **materialized** onto the table.

Manya stepped forward, reaching out to pick it up. The cover was cracked and faded, whispering of years long past.

She flipped it open, curiosity burning inside her. "Guys, look! I found a strange diary. It's quite old…"

Her words were cut off abruptly.

Before Vanshika and Naina could react, Manya vanished.

A stunned silence filled the room.

"Manya?! Where did she go?!" Vanshika's voice trembled.

Naina rushed forward, panic tightening her throat. "What happened?! Where is she?! And what is this diary?!"

Her hands trembled as she picked up the book. She barely turned a page before horror twisted her expression, and she threw the diary across the table.

Vanshika grabbed her shoulders. "What happened?!"

Naina swallowed hard before whispering, "Look at the last page..."

Vanshika cautiously stepped forward and flipped to the end.

There, glaring back at them, was a *blood-stained* message.

Below the message was a picture of Manya; her expression frozen in shock.

Scrawled in deep crimson ink, the words *"I'VE CAPTURED MANYA. I WILL RISE." burned into the page like a dark omen.*

A chill settled over them.

Mini rushed in at that moment, sensing the tension. "What's going on?!"

Vanshika pointed toward the diary, unable to form the words. Mini picked it up, her eyes widening.

She paled.

"This... this isn't just any diary." Her voice wavered. "It belongs to... an ancient sorcerer, the one who has long been forgotten by most. Veyron."

Naina gasped. "Veyron?! The same one whose curse we accidentally broke two years ago?!"

Mini nodded gravely. "Yes. And now... he's back. And he has Manya."

A tense silence filled the room before Mini straightened, determination flashing in her eyes.

"We have no time to waste. We're going to get Manya back. But this time, we're facing an enemy unlike any we've encountered before."

Vanshika **clenched** her fist. "Then we fight. We're protectors now we can't let him win."

Naina nodded. "We're ready. We won't let her down."

Mini exhaled, nodding. "Then let's begin. We're going after Veyron."

As the air thickened with the weight of their mission, the wands in their hands pulsed, ready to **wield** magic like never before.

Their greatest battle had begun.

THE END

Enchanted Definations

THE MYSTERIOUS PORTAL

1. **SORCERESS** → witch
2. **KNOWING SMILE** → wise smirk
3. **BRIMMING** ▸ overflowing
4. **EERIE GLASS CASE** ▸ spooky display
5. **PARCHMENT** → paper, scroll
6. **GAZE** → stare
7. **FRAGMENT** → piece
8. **DRIFTED** → floated
9. **INTRICATE** → complex, detailed
10. **ALIGNED** → positioned, arranged
11. **AIR THICKENED** ▸ tension rose
12. **RADIANT** → glowing
13. **SWIRLING** ▸ spinning, whirling
14. **HYPNOTIC** → mesmerizing
15. **WARPED** → distorted, twisted
16. **RIPPLING** → waving, undulating

AN UNKNOWN GUEST

1. **SHIMMERED** → glowed, sparkled
2. **CRACKLED** → snapped, popped
3. **GUST** → blast, burst
4. **RUSTLING** → swishing, whispering
5. **FLICKER WILDLY** → flash erratically
6. **RIFT** → gap, split
7. **ASTONISHED** → amazed
8. **DARTING** → quick-moving, rushing
9. **BRUSHED OFF** → ignored, dismissed
10. **LINGERED** → stayed, remained
11. **HESITANTLY** → unsurely

12. **WELLED UP** → rose, filled
13. **BEWILDERED** → confused, puzzled
14. **INSTINCTIVELY** → automatically
15. **GEMSTONE** → jewel
16. **SHIVERS** ▸ chills, tremors
17. **DARKENING** ▸ fading, dimming
18. **REALM** ▸ kingdom, world
19. **ACCUSED** ▸ blamed, charged
20. **GROWL** ▸ snarl, rumble
21. **MORTAL** ▸ human, earthly
22. **SWORN** ▸ promised, vowed
23. **TAINTED** ▸ corrupted, spoiled
24. **WEILDING** ▸ holding, using
25. **INSATIABLE** ▸ greedy, never satisfied
26. **LACED** ▸ threaded, intertwined
27. **MENACE** ▸ threat, danger
28. **DEFY** ▸ challenge
29. **RESIST** ▸ oppose, refuse
30. **ULTIMATUM** ▸ last chance
31. **YIELD** ▸ give in, surrender
32. **FORGED** ▸ created
33. **RAGED** ▸ stormed
34. **MAYHEM** ▸ chaos
35. **OUNCE** ▸ small amount
36. **COMPREHEND** ▸ understand, grasp
37. **CONFRONTED** ▸ faced, challenged
38. **CONTORTING** ▸ twisting, bending
39. **FLEETING** ▸ short-lived, temporary
40. **PRECISE** ▸ exact, accurate
41. **UNRAVELING** ▸ falling apart
42. **HEART RACING** ▸ excited, anxious
43. **SNAPPING** ▸ breaking, cracking
44. **CLUTCHES** → grips

THE SISTERS' REUNION

1. **DAWN** → sunrise
2. **CONFINES** → limits
3. **SURREAL** → unreal, dreamlike
4. **STARTLED** → shocked, surprised
5. **ETCHED** → carved, engraved
6. **TINGED** → shaded, colored
7. **ELATED** → thrilled, happy
8. **DISMISSIVELY** → carelessly
9. **SHACKLES** → chains
10. **PROMPTLY** → quickly, immediately
11. **CHIME** → ring, sound
12. **TRINKETS**▸ small ornaments, charms

GIRLS AND MAGIC

1. **SWIRL** → spin, twist
2. **ERUPTED** ▸ exploded
3. **PALPABLE** → obvious
4. **METICULOUSLY** ▸ carefully
5. **HALT** → stop
6. **GLINT** → sparkle, shine
7. **ORNATE** ▸ decorated, elaborate
8. **ATTUNED** → in sync, connected
9. **BEAMED** → smiled, shone
10. **ENIGMATIC** → mysterious
11. **INTUITIVE** → natural, instinctive
12. **AWRY** → wrong
13. **OMEN** → sign, warning

Protectors of the Magical Court

1. **WHIRLWIND** → fast-moving, stormy
2. **MOMENTOUS**→important, significant
3. **MATERIALIZED** → appeared, formed
4. **CLENCHED** → gripped, tightened

5. **WIELD** → handle, use

Author's Note

I hope you have loved your journey through the chapters. In the thrilling sequels, girls embarks on an epic journey to save Manya. Facing danger, uncovering secrets, and forging unbreakable bonds, their courage will redefine destiny.
-Naisha Sahni

www.ingramcontent.com/pod-product-compliance
Lightning Source LLC
Chambersburg PA
CBHW021147130726
47988CB00004B/1495